Old Mother Goose

when she wanted to wander,
Would ride through the air
on a very fine gander.

WILLIAM

WEGMAN'S

MOTHER

GOOSE

Hyperion · New York

WHAT DOES MOTHER GOOSE DO WHEN
SHE ISN'T WANDERING AROUND IN THE SKY ON HER GANDER?

She stays home and makes up rhymes to entertain herself and her children.

The rhymes she likes most, she writes down in her book.

These are some of her favorites...

★

JACK

COCK-CROW

THE TEN O'CLOCK SCHOLAR

OLD MOTHER HUBBARD

LITTLE JACK HORNER

OLD KING COLE

COFFEE AND TEA

JACK AND JILL

FINGERS AND TOES

LITTLE JUMPING JOAN

THREE MEN IN A TUB

LITTLE MISS MUFFET

LUCY LOCKET

LITTLE BO-PEEP

MASTER I HAVE

PAT-A-CAKE

THIS LITTLE PIGGY

JACK SPRAT

LITTLE BOY BLUE

JACK

Jack be
nimble,

Jack be
quick,

Jack jump over the
candlestick.

COCK-CROW

Cocks crow
in the morn
To tell us to rise,
And he who lies late
Will never be wise;

For early to bed
And early to rise,
Is the way to be
healthy,
wealthy,
and wise.

THE TEN O'CLOCK SCHOLAR

"Perhaps you overslept. Get to bed earlier."

(See "Cock-Crow," previous page.)

A diller, a dollar,

A ten o'clock scholar!

What makes you come so soon?

You used to come at ten o'clock,

But now you come at

noon.

Who do you think is older, Mother Hubbard or her dog?

Old Mother Hubbard went to her cupboard,

OLD

To give her poor dog a bone;

MOTHER

But when she got there the cupboard was bare,

HUBBARD

And so the poor dog had none.

Make sure to have plenty of bones for your dog. (Mother Hubbard also enjoys bones.)

Little Jack Horner

HOW MANY WORDS CAN

YOU THINK OF

THAT RHYME WITH PLUM...

OTHER THAN THUMB?

HOW ABOUT HORNER...

OTHER THAN CORNER?

Little Jack Horner sat in the corner,

Eating a Christmas pie:

He put in his thumb and pulled out a plum.

And said, "What a good boy am I!"

OLD KING COLE

Old King Cole

Was a merry old soul,

And a merry old soul was he;

He called for his pipe,

And he called for his bowl,

And he called for his fiddlers three!

And every fiddler, he had a fine fiddle,

And a very fine fiddle had he.

"Twee tweedle dee, tweedle dee," went the fiddlers.

Oh, there's none so rare

As can compare

With King Cole and his fiddlers three.

COFFEE AND TEA

Molly, my sister, and I fell out,
And what do you think it was all about?
She loved coffee and I loved tea,
And that was the reason we couldn't agree.

(Mother Goose likes to mix the two.)

JACK AND JILL

JACK AND JILL
WENT UP
THE HILL,
TO FETCH
A PAIL OF
WATER;
JACK FELL
DOWN,
AND BROKE
HIS CROWN,
AND JILL
CAME
TUMBLING
AFTER.

As we climb higher the air becomes thinner, which can make us dizzy. Be careful of running at high altitudes.

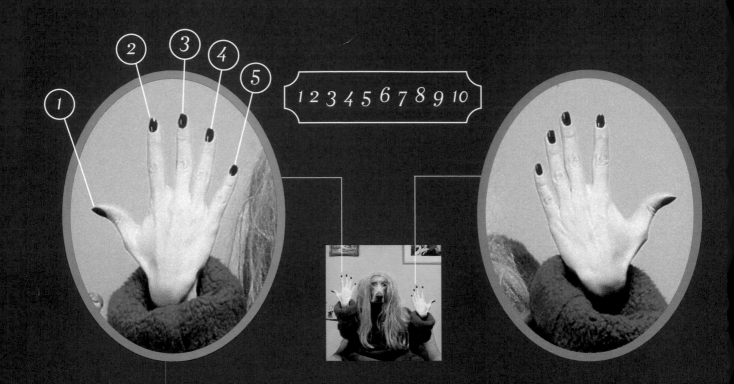

1 2 3 4 5 6 7 8 9 10

FINGERS AND TOES

Every lady in this land has twenty nails. Upon each hand
Five, and twenty on hands and feet. All this is true, without deceit.

11 12 13 14 15 + 5 = 20

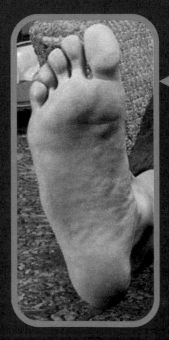

LITTLE JUMPING JOAN

Here am I,
little jumping Joan.
When nobody's with me
I'm always
alone.

LITTLE JUMPING JOAN

Here am I,
little jumping Joan.
When nobody's with me
I'm always
alone.

When not jumping with Joan, Joan is jumping with Jack.

Rub
a-dub-dub, Three men in a tub

And who do you think they be?

The butcher, the baker,

the candlestick-maker;

Turn 'em out, knaves all three!

Aye... Where's the rub? Do you think they should be in the tub at the same time? Do you think they should be in the tub with their clothes on?

Little
Miss
Muffet
Sat
on
a
tuffet,
Eating
her
curds
and
whey;
.
.
.
Along
came
a
spider,
And
sat
down
beside
her,
And
frightened
Miss
Muffet
away.
.
.
.
.
.
.
.

Little Miss Muffet

How in the world does one lose one's pocket? Leave it to Lucy...

LUCY
LOCKET

*Lucy Locket
lost her pocket,
Kitty Fisher found it;
Nothing in it,
nothing in it,
But the binding
round it.*

L

ittle Bo-Peep

Little Bo-Peep has lost her sheep,
And can't tell where to find them;
Leave them alone, and they'll come home,
And bring their tails behind them.

"Where _are_ those sheep?"

Master I

Master I have,
and I am his man,
Gallop a dreary dun;

Master I have,
and I am his man,
And I'll get a wife
as fast as I can;

With a heighty gaily
gamberally,
Higgledy piggledy,
niggledy, niggledy,
Gallop a dreary dun.

Have

Pat-a-cake, pat-a-cake,

baker's man!

Bake me a cake as fast

as you can.

Pat it

and PAT-A-CAKE

prick

it and

mark it with a *B*,

And put it in the

oven for Baby and me.

THIS LITTLE PIGGY

This little piggy

went to market;

This little piggy

stayed at home;

This little piggy

had roast beef;

This little piggy

had none;

This little piggy

said,
"Wee, wee, wee, wee!"

All the way home.

JACK SPRAT

Jack Sprat

could eat

no fat.

His wife

could eat

no lean;

And so

between

them both,

They licked

the platter

clean.

Mother Goose
reminds you to eat
more vegetables.

L

ITTLE BOY BLUE,

come, blow your horn!

The sheep's in the meadow,

the cow's in the corn.

Where's the little boy

that looks after the sheep?

Under the haystack,

fast asleep!

*It's okay to take
naps, but not when you
are on duty.*

For information address
Hyperion Books for Children, 114 Fifth Avenue, New York, New York, 10011-5690.

First Edition
1 3 5 7 9 10 8 6 4 2
Library of Congress Cataloging-in-Publication Data
Wegman, William.
Wegman's Mother Goose/by William Wegman. —1st ed.
p.   cm.
Summary: A collection of classic nursery rhymes illustrated with photographs
of Weimaraner dogs portraying the storybook characters.
ISBN 0-7868-0218-9 (trade) — ISBN 0-7868-2231-7 (lib. bdg.)
1. Nursery rhymes. 2. Children's poetry. [1. Nursery rhymes.] I.Title.
PZ8.3.W414We 1996
398'.8 — dc20
96-1425

Design: Drenttel Doyle Partners.

This book is set in Bureau Grotesque, Cochin, Didot, Doyle Didot, Industrial, Interstate,
Kuenstler Script, Linoscript, MatrixScript, News Gothic, Officina Sans, Poetica,
Scala, Snell, Spectrum, Trade Gothic, Wallpaper Cut & Paste-script, amongst others.

ACKNOWLEDGMENTS

WITH THANKS TO: *Andrea Beeman, Jason Burch, Christine Burgin, Drenttel Doyle Partners,*
John Enman, Patricia Fay, Arnaldo Hernandez, The New York Kunsthalle, Martin Kunz, Asia Linn,
Suzanne Lipschutz, Dave McMillan, The Pace/MacGill Gallery, Tamsin Raikes,
Carleen Ramkime, Howard Reeves, Victoria Sambonaris, John Slyce, Small Furniture, Samuel O. J. Spivey
and Alexandra Anderson-Spivey, Katleen Sterck, Bob Vissicchio, and Pam Wegman

THE CAST: *Battina, Chip, Chundo, and Crooky*
Old Mother Hubbard's Dog: Buster Miller   Little Piggies: The litter of BD and GD
HANDS AND FEET: *Andrea Beeman, Jason Burch, Christine Burgin, John Slyce, and Pam Wegman*
PHOTOGRAPH PRINTING: *Terry Rozo and Katleen Sterck*
ENDPAPER PHOTOGRAPHS: *Jason Burch, Arnaldo Hernandez*